EDITOR'S NOTE: The original idea for the story of SWAN LAKE was based on themes from an eighteenth century tale DER GERAUBTE SCHLEIER by J.K.A. Musaeus. His rather ornate story has been adapted considerably over the years, and the version used by Tchaikovsky in the familiar and beloved ballet is quite different from the original. The version in this book differs slightly from either of these sources in having a happy ending in which love triumphs over evil, an ending that also appears in some of the earlier variants of the story. The story has been retold in English for this edition by Anthea Bell.

Illustrations copyright © 1984, Takeshi Matsumoto
Original Japanese edition published in 1984 by Kodansha Ltd., Tokyo.
English text copyright © 1986, Neugebauer Press, London–Boston.
Published by PICTURE BOOK STUDIO, an imprint of Neugebauer Press.
Distributed in USA by Alphabet Press, Natick, MA.
Distributed in Canada by Vanwell Publishing, St. Catharines, Ont.
Distributed in U.K. by Ragged Bears, Andover.
Distributed in Australia by Hodder and Stoughton Australia Pty, Ltd.
All rights reserved.
Printed in Austria.

LIBRARY OF CONGRESS CATALOGING IN PUBLICATION DATA

Bell, Anthea.
Swan lake.

Adaption of Tchaikovsky's Lebedinoe ozero.
Summary: A prince's love for a swan queen overcomes an evil sorcerer's spell in this fairy tale adaption of the classic ballet.
[1. Ballets—Stories, plots, etc. 2. Fairy tales]
I. Iwasaki, Chihiro, 1918-1974, ill.
II. Tchaikovsky, Peter Ilich, 1840-1893, Lebedinoe ozero. III. Title.
PZ8.B399Sw   1986   [E]   86-9509

ISBN 0-88708-028-6

Ask your bookseller for these other PICTURE BOOK STUDIO books illustrated by Chihiro Iwasaki:
THE RED SHOES by Hans Christian Andersen
THE LITTLE MERMAID by Hans Christian Andersen
SNOW WHITE AND THE SEVEN DWARVES by the Brothers Grimm
THE WISE QUEEN by Anthea Bell

Swan Lake

A Traditional Folktale retold by Anthea Bell · Illustrated by Chihiro Iwasaki

PICTURE BOOK STUDIO

There was once a handsome young Prince called Siegfried who lived in a great castle in a forest. The Prince would soon come of age, and on his birthday a ball was to be held at which he would choose a girl to be his wife.

As the birthday drew near, all the Prince's people prepared to rejoice and make merry, but he himself was deep in thought as he walked in the forest. Princesses were coming to the ball from far and wide, and yet he neither knew, nor loved any of them. How could he possibly make his choice of a bride?

As he walked among the trees he came to a lake, and a flock of wild swans passed overhead. The beautiful white birds flew down to settle on the waters of the lake, and the Prince saw, to his amazement, that one of them wore a golden crown.

The Prince snatched up his bow and bent it to shoot this strange and beautiful swan. At that very moment, however, the swans turned into lovely girls.

The most beautiful of them all was wearing the golden crown. "Tell me your name, lovely maiden!" the Prince begged her.

"My name is Odette, Prince Siegfried," she said, "and I was once the Princess of a distant country, but an evil enchanter bewitched me and cast a spell on me and my companions. We take on human form again at nightfall, but during the day we are birds, and must fly in the air or swim on the water in the shape of swans."

"Is there no way to break this spell?" cried the Prince.

"Why, yes," said Odette. "If a handsome Prince were to love me and make me his wife, then I should be freed from the enchantment." The Prince was delighted to hear this; nothing could be easier, he thought, for he had fallen in love with the beautiful swan maiden at first sight, and she had fallen in love with him as well. "Come to the ball at the castle tomorrow night," he told her, "and I will choose you as my bride. Then the spell will be broken and you will be free!"

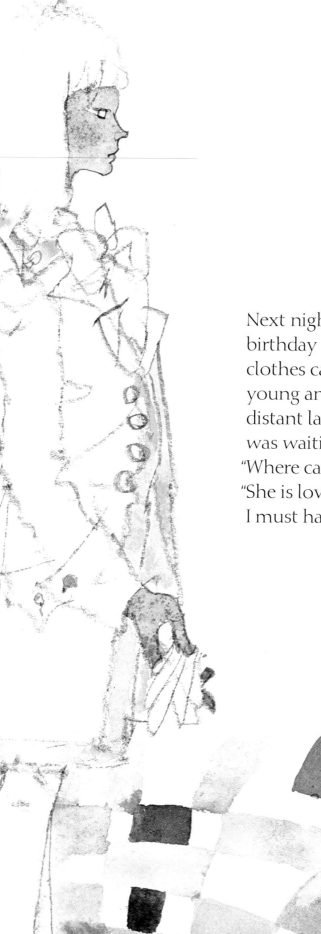

Next night the great ball for the Prince's birthday was held. Guests in magnificent clothes came driving up, among them young and lovely Princesses from many distant lands. Yet all the time, the Prince was waiting eagerly for his beloved Odette. "Where can she be?" he wondered. "She is lovelier than the moon itself, and I must have her for my wife!"

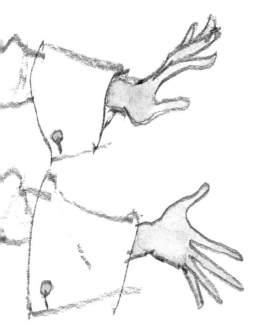

Then a fanfare of trumpets sounded, and
another Princess entered the great hall:
a girl of wonderful beauty who looked just
like Odette, and was dressed all in black.
"You are here at last!" cried the Prince joyfully,
going to meet her. "This girl and no other
shall be my bride!" he told his courtiers.

They were all delighted that their Prince
had chosen a wife, and the dancing began.

But as they all made merry, a beautiful white swan appeared outside
one of the windows, beating its wings against the glass and crying sadly,
"Prince Siegfried, the evil enchanter has deceived you! I am your Odette,
and now that you have chosen another as your wife the spell can never
be broken!"
And when the Prince ran to look out of the window, he saw the swan
flying away.
"Then who are you?" he asked, turning to the Princess in black.

"I am the enchanter's daughter, changed into the likeness of Odette by his
magic arts," said the girl in black, "and you have promised to marry me!"

At that there came a great gust
of wind and a mighty clap of thunder,
darkness filled the hall, and the evil enchanter
himself appeared in the form of a dreadful demon.

"You fool, Prince Siegfried!" he cried in a great and terrible voice.
"You are my daughter's now, and you cannot break my spell!"
And the enchanter's dreadful laughter rang out in the darkness.

"No!" cried the Prince, rushing towards the place where he heard the enchanter's voice. "You shall die!" So saying, he drew his sword and thrust it into the monstrous shape of the demon with all his might. The enchanter screamed horribly and fell to the ground dying, cursing the Prince.
"You may kill me," he cried, "but the spell upon Odette and her companions can never be broken. Remember that!"

Beside the lake, the swan maidens were waiting happily to hear the news that the Prince had chosen Odette as his wife, when they would all be freed from their enchantment. "Once Odette has married her Prince we shall never be swans again!" they cried.

But then Odette herself appeared, pale as Death. "The Prince chose the enchanter's daughter for his bride instead of me," she said sadly, "and now the spell cannot be broken."

The Prince himself now came running down to the lake,
desperate to find his lost Odette.
"I have killed the evil enchanter!" he cried.

"Alas, but the spell still binds me," said Odette.
"I hoped to return to human form and be your wife,
but now there is no hope for me!" And weeping bitterly,
she ran to the shores of the lake and threw herself into
its waters.
"Wait for me, Odette!" cried the Prince.
"I will come with you. I would rather drown with you
than marry the enchanter's daughter."
Clasped in each other's arms, the lovers sank to the
bottom of the lake, while the weeping swan maidens
lamented.

But even as they mourned for the lost lovers, a wonderful light began to shine, and a boat shaped like a great shell rose to the surface of the water, with the Prince and Odette standing in it.
The strength of their love had broken the spell, and the evil enchanter's power was destroyed forever.